For Bernard who loves gardens — F.W.

To my little Simona — F.N.

THIS IS A BORZOI BOOK PUBLISHED BY ALFRED A. KNOPF, INC.
Text copyright © 1999 by Fiona Waters.
Illustrations copyright © 1999 by Fabian Negrin.
All rights reserved under International
and Pan-American Copyright Conventions.
Published in the United States by Alfred A. Knopf, Inc., New York, and
simultaneously in Canada by Random House
of Canada Limited, Toronto.
Distributed by Random House, Inc., New York.
Originally published in Great Britain in 1999
by Bloomsbury Children's Books.
KNOPF, BORZOI BOOKS, and the colophon are
registered trademarks of Random House, Inc.

www.randomhouse.com/kids

Library of Congress Cataloging-in-Publication Data
Waters, Fiona.
Oscar Wilde's The selfish giant / retold by Fiona Waters ; illustrated by
Fabian Negrin.
p. cm.
Summary: A once selfish giant welcomes the children to his previously
forbidden garden and is eventually rewarded by an unusual little child.
ISBN 0-375-80319-X (trade). — ISBN 0-375-90319-4 (lib. bdg.)
[1. Fairy tales. 2. Giants—Fiction.] I. Negrin, Fabian, ill. II. Wilde,
Oscar, 1854–1900. Selfish giant. III. Title.
PZ8.W280s 2000
[Fic]—dc21   99-32495

Printed in Hong Kong
First American Edition: February 2000

10 9 8 7 6 5 4 3 2 1

OSCAR WILDE'S
THE SELFISH GIANT

Retold by FIONA WATERS

Illustrated by FABIAN NEGRIN

ALFRED A. KNOPF, *New York*

The garden was large and slightly wild. The deep lush grass was scattered with little white starry daisies, and bluebells and buttercups bloomed in all the corners. Butterflies sunned themselves on the carpets of flowers and the thyme hummed with buzzing bees. In the spring the twelve old peach trees were covered with pale pink blossoms, and later in the year the branches would bend to the ground, laden with delicious fruits. The air was filled with the sweetest of sounds as the birds sang the day long, and then in the evening they would fall silent as the nightingale began her evening serenade.

Every afternoon the children used to creep into the garden on their way home from school. They would make daisy chains and play hide-and-seek in amongst the bushes. They lay on their backs in the grass and looked up into the spreading branches of the trees, and they sang along with the birds. They all loved the garden and the garden loved them.

Now the garden belonged to the Giant. Long before any of the children could remember, he had gone off to Cornwall to visit his friend the Ogre and had somehow managed to stay for seven years. Eventually they decided they had said all they wanted to say to each other and the Giant took his leave, thanking the Ogre for his hospitality. He strode back to his castle and discovered the children playing in his garden.

"Who said you could come into my garden?" he roared in his very deep gruff voice. "How dare you disturb me with your noise!"

The children were absolutely terrified, as the Giant was so very big and his voice so very fierce. They all fled down the path and away as fast as their legs could carry them.

"This is my garden and I want it all to myself. No one else shall be allowed to come in, especially not noisy children," the Giant muttered to himself.

The very next day he built a great high brick wall all around the garden, so high no one could even see in, and he put up a notice that read:

TRESPASSERS
WILL BE
PROSECUTED

The children came skipping down the road after school only to discover the dreadful wall. They couldn't even catch a glimpse of the beautiful garden or hear the birds singing. Now they had nowhere to play. Their mothers scolded them for getting in their way while they were busy.

The roads outside the garden were hard and dusty and full of sharp stones and there were no butterflies. The children could only walk around and around the high wall, talking sadly about how happy they had been in the beautiful garden.

The Giant was a very selfish giant.

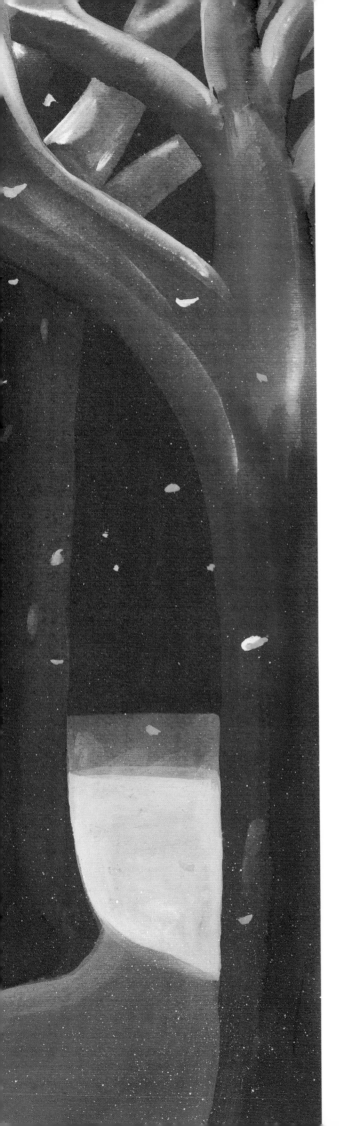

Time passed, and all the while the Selfish Giant's garden grew to be a sadder and sadder place. The birds no longer sang and the flowers withered away. There were no blossoms on the peach trees that Spring. Frost and Snow lived there all the time. Snow covered everything with her deep cold blanket, and Frost encased all the trees with her hard and bitter ice. Soon the North Wind joined them and he blew all day, sending icy drafts into the corners of the Selfish Giant's castle. And on his breath came Hail, drumming on the rooftops.

"Spring is very late this year," pondered the Selfish Giant as he sat gloomily by the window looking out at his wasted garden. "I do hope the weather improves soon. I want to walk in the lush green grass and look at the bluebells and buttercups again."

But Winter never loosened his grip, and only the North Wind and Hail and Snow and Frost played in the garden that had once rung with the merry shouts of the children. The Selfish Giant grew sad, but he did not remove his stern notice or take down the high brick wall.

One morning as the Selfish Giant lay huddled in his great bed trying to keep warm, he suddenly heard the most lovely music. It was so sweet and pure he thought it was the most beautiful sound he had ever heard, and he was sure the King's Musicians must be marching by. He leapt out of bed, scattering rugs and blankets as he strode to open the window to hear the music better.

But there was no great parade of courtiers, only a little brown bird, a linnet, singing on a branch of one of the old peach trees. It was so long since he had heard a bird singing that he had forgotten how beautiful it could sound. A marvelous perfume came wafting in through the window and the Selfish Giant cried out, "I do believe Spring has finally come back!" And he looked out at his garden.

And what do you think he saw?

He saw the most wonderful sight. Spring had indeed returned to his sad garden, and so had the children. They had found a small hole in the great high wall and they had crept in like tiny little mice. They were all sitting on the branches of the trees, and the trees were so delighted to have the children back that they were covered in gently dancing leaves and pale pink blossoms. Every tree had a laughing child in its branches, and the birds were swooping here, there, and everywhere in their delight.

Of Winter and Hail and Frost and Snow and the bitter cold North Wind there was no sign.

Except in one far corner. There the Snow was still piled up, the North Wind was still huffing and puffing, and the tree that stood there was quite bare—no dancing leaves, no gentle blossoms, no birds singing. And as the Selfish Giant peered out of his window, he realized why.

At the foot of the tree stood a little boy who was too tiny to climb up onto a branch. The tree bent its branches as low as possible, but the boy was too small.

And as he looked out the window, the Selfish Giant realized just how terribly selfish he had been and how much he had missed the happy children and the joy they brought to his garden. He realized that it was his fault that Spring had never returned to the garden and he was truly sorry for what he had done.

He ran down the winding stairs and straight out into the garden to
help the little boy up into the branches of the Winter-bound tree. But as
soon as the children saw him they turned and fled because they were
still very frightened of him, and as they ran the garden turned to Winter
again. Only the little boy remained. His eyes were so full of tears that he
did not see the Giant as he walked toward him.

The Giant bent down and, very gently, picked up the little boy and placed him high up in the branches of the tree. The tree burst into blossom and the birds swooped down singing, and the little boy wrapped his tiny arms around the Giant's great neck and kissed him.

When the other children saw that the Giant wasn't cross and grumpy anymore, they all came back into the garden in a great rush and with them came Spring! The Giant gathered the children around him and said, "It is your garden now, children. You must come and play here whenever you want. The garden will be full of love and laughter and happiness, and you are all very welcome."

The Giant then knocked down the great high brick wall and threw away the sign that said:

TRESPASSERS WILL BE PROSECUTED

All day long the children played, their happy shouts echoing around the garden. When their parents came looking for them anxiously in the evening, they found them all sitting with the Giant in the most beautiful garden there had ever been. And the Giant's face was wreathed in smiles.

As the children came to say good-bye, promising to come again the next day, the Giant asked them all in turn if they had seen the smallest boy, the one he had helped into the tree.

"If you see him, please do tell him to come back with you. I should so like to see him again," said the Giant. But no one seemed to know him, and the Giant was very sad, for he loved him the best.

From that time on the children came every afternoon after school to play in the Giant's garden, and he was always there with them, joining in the games and the laughter, and the garden grew more and more beautiful. The children would make huge daisy chains to hang around the Giant's neck and weave garlands of flowers around his enormous head. They would climb all over his long, long legs as he sat on the grass, and he would carry them around the garden, high on his shoulders, where they felt they could touch the stars.

For the Giant there was only one sadness. The little boy he loved never came again. He always asked the children if they had seen him, but the answer was always the same. No one knew him or where he lived or indeed where he had come from. The Giant longed to see him and would often speak of him.

Years passed, and the Giant grew old and his hair grew gray. His bones grew stiff and he could no longer join in all the games, but he carried a huge armchair into the garden and would watch the children playing.

"There are many beautiful flowers in my garden, but the children are the most beautiful of all," he said. He was no longer called the Selfish Giant, and everyone loved him very much. He watched the seasons changing but never minded Winter now, as he knew Spring would not be far behind.

One cold, snowy day he looked out of the window onto the garden and rubbed his eyes in surprise. He knew his eyesight was failing, but it looked to him as if a corner of the garden had blossoms on the trees. He clambered stiffly down the winding stairs and out into the garden. Strangely, he didn't seem to feel the cold, although there was snow on the ground and the wind was icy. He walked slowly across the grass. His eyes were not deceiving him. In the farthest corner one of the old peach trees was covered in glorious white blossoms. The leaves were golden, and heavy silver fruit hung down from the branches. But most wondrous of all, underneath the tree stood his first little friend, the boy he had helped into the very same tree all those years ago. The Giant spread his arms wide and came close to the child, but then he stopped in great anger for he saw that the child had two wounds on the palms of his hands and two in his little feet. They were the prints of nails.

"Who has dared to do this to you?" the Giant rumbled. "Tell me and I will slay him with my great ax. Who has dared to harm you?"

But the child just smiled at the great angry Giant and said, "Do not be angry, dear Giant. These are the wounds of Love."

The Giant fell to his knees as he looked at the radiant child. "Who are you?" he murmured as he felt a great sense of awe overcoming him.

The child just smiled again and laid his small hand with the ugly wound on the Giant's shoulder. "A long time ago you let me play in your garden. Now I have come to take you to my garden, which is called Paradise."

And when the children ran into the garden that afternoon, they found their dear friend the Giant lying dead under the tree, all covered in white blossoms and with a gentle smile on his old face.